If You Believe!

Sheila Mayo

ISBN 978-1-0980-6153-1 (hardcover)
ISBN 978-1-0980-6154-8 (digital)

Christian Faith Publishing, Inc.
832 Park Avenue
Meadville, PA 16335
www.christianfaithpublishing.com

Printed in the United States of America

Dedication

This book is dedicated to the glory of God's love and to my children, Lauren and Marshall for their love and support and who never cease to be my champions. And last but not least my sweet pup, Helios who reminds me how important it is to stop and play every day!

Daniel is a caterpillar who lives on a lemon tree. *Today is a great day!* Daniel thinks. The sun is shining, the birds are singing, and he has this wonderful lemon tree to enjoy.

Suddenly, a shadow appears. Daniel looks up and sees a beautiful blanket of color. Daniel is surprised! He wonders what this could be. Daniel calls out to the shadow, but it flutters past him. He watches the colorful shadow as it flies up and down, touching each flower as it goes along.

That night, as the sun sets and Daniel gets comfortable for the evening, he tries to sleep. The moon is high, and the breeze gently sways him. This helps Daniel to fall asleep. He dreams of the beautiful colors that he saw today fluttering by.

The next morning, as the birds begin to chirp and the sun begins to shine, Daniel awakens hungry as he always does. He begins to eat faster, and he eats more that in the days before. Daniel notices that he is getting bigger and stronger.

Daniel watches for the colorful shadow, hoping it will stop and visit with him today. Daniel is happy for his home and for the beautiful day. Daniel sees many of his friends. A snail passes by.

A cricket says hello, a ladybug stops by, and Daniel sees a red bird.

The day is almost over.

Daniel is hopeful that he will see the shadow. Just as he is about to give up, the colorful shadow appears. It floats over him, back and forth as if to be saying, "Hello, let me look at you." Then it is gone as fast as it came.

Bedtime! Daniel can hardly sleep. He is very excited! Daniel dreams of a special time. He dreams that he is floating along with the beautiful blanket of color. He is happy!

The next day, before the sun comes up, Daniel has eaten two times more than before. He feels excited for the day. Something in his heart tells him that today he will meet the colorful floating beauty.

Daniel begins watching as soon as the sun comes up. Wait!
Daniel sees a shadow! Oh, it's a bee! The bee stops to visit.
Daniel tells the bee about the colorful shadow he has seen. The
bee explains, "She is a butterfly." Before Daniel can ask what a
butterfly is, the bee has flown away.

A butterfly, he thinks. Just as Daniel begins eating his lemon leaves again, a surprise! There she is, the beautiful butterfly! She flutters all around him. Daniel is so excited! He wants to look at her. Will she ever be still? The butterfly finally stops and lands.

The butterfly smiles at him. She tells him the story of how she was once a caterpillar just like him. The butterfly tells Daniel that she knew in her heart that she was meant for great things. She believed that she could be a butterfly.

Daniel smiled and told the butterfly that he too wanted to believe in his heart that he could be a butterfly, and so he did!

Remember, you have everything you need inside of you to be all that God created you to be if you believe!

About the Author

Sheila Mayo is a native Texan who lives with her Goldendoodle, Helios, and is the proud mother of two children. Sheila has always wanted to write books for children, and now more than ever she feels that we need positive messages for our younger generations. This is the beginning of her journey with a great message to tell young readers all over the world! When Sheila is not writing for young children, you will find her working as VP of a company, playing with her sweet pup, donating to causes dear to her heart for children and nature conservation, painting murals, and—her favorite—spending time with her now adult children and their families, cooking together and sharing a great meal.

CPSIA information can be obtained
at www.ICGtesting.com
Printed in the USA
LVHW070428130721
692524LV00005B/31

9 781098 061531